Quentin Blake

MISTER MAGNOLIA

TED SMART

MISTER MAGNOLIA

This edition produced for The Book People Ltd,
Hall Wood Avenue, Haydock, St Helens, WA11 9UL

First published in Great Britain by Jonathan Cape,
an imprint of Random House Children's Books

Jonathan Cape edition published 1980
The Book People edition published 2006

1 3 5 7 9 10 8 6 4 2

Copyright © Quentin Blake, 1980

The right of Quentin Blake
to be identified as the author and illustrator of this work
has been asserted in accordance with the Copyright, Designs and Patents Act 1988.

RANDOM HOUSE CHILDREN'S BOOKS
61–63 Uxbridge Road, London W5 5SA
A division of The Random House Group Ltd

RANDOM HOUSE AUSTRALIA (PTY) LTD
20 Alfred Street, Milsons Point, Sydney,
New South Wales 2061, Australia

RANDOM HOUSE NEW ZEALAND LTD
18 Poland Road, Glenfield, Auckland 10, New Zealand

RANDOM HOUSE (PTY) LTD
Isle of Houghton, Corner Boundary Road & Carse O'Gowrie,
Houghton 2198, South Africa

RANDOM HOUSE INDIA PVT LTD
301 World Trade Tower, Hotel Intercontinental Grand Complex,
Barakhamba Lane, New Delhi 110001, India

THE RANDOM HOUSE GROUP Limited Reg. No. 954009

A CIP catalogue record for this book is available from the British Library.

Printed in China

Mr Magnolia has only one boot.

He has an old trumpet

that goes rooty-toot —

And two lovely sisters
who play on the flute —

But Mr Magnolia has only one boot.

In his pond live a frog

and a toad and a newt —

He has green parakeets

who pick holes in his suit —

And some very fat owls
who are learning to hoot —
But Mr Magnolia
has only one boot.

He gives rides to his friends

when he goes for a scoot —

And the splash is immense
when he comes down
the chute —

But Mr Magnolia
has only one boot.

Just look at the way that
he juggles with fruit!

The mice all march past
as he takes the salute!

And his dinosaur!

What a MAGNIFICENT

brute!

But Mr Magnolia —
poor Mr Magnolia!
— Mr Magnolia
has
only one boot . . .

Hey —

Wait a minute . . .

Now then . . .

Keep going . . .

What's this?

Look!

It's a boot!

It's a boot!

Whoopee
for Mr Magnolia's
new boot!

Good night.